INFINITY

IN THE GAME!

Adapted by Courtney Carbone

A Random House PICTUREBACK® Book

Random House New York

 Published in the United States by Random House Children's Books, a division of Random House LLC, 1745 Broadway, New York, NY 10019, and in Canada by Random House of Canada Limited, Toronto, Penguin Random House Companies, in conjunction with Disney Enterprises, Inc.

randomhouse.com/kids ISBN 978-0-7364-3269-6 MANUFACTURED IN CHINA

10 9 8 7 6 5 4 3 2 1

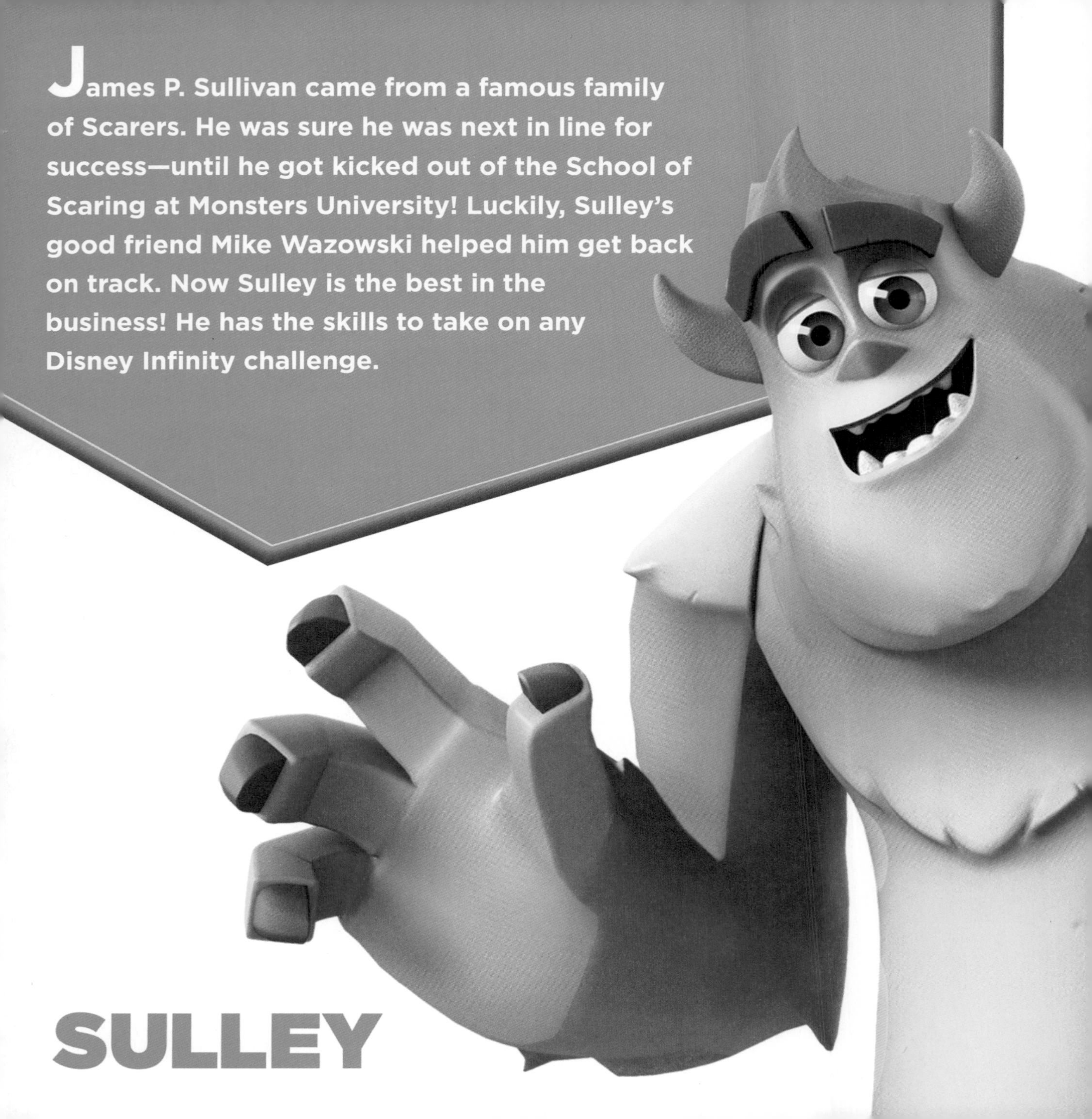

James P. Sullivan came from a famous family of Scarers. He was sure he was next in line for success—until he got kicked out of the School of Scaring at Monsters University! Luckily, Sulley's good friend Mike Wazowski helped him get back on track. Now Sulley is the best in the business! He has the skills to take on any Disney Infinity challenge.

SULLEY

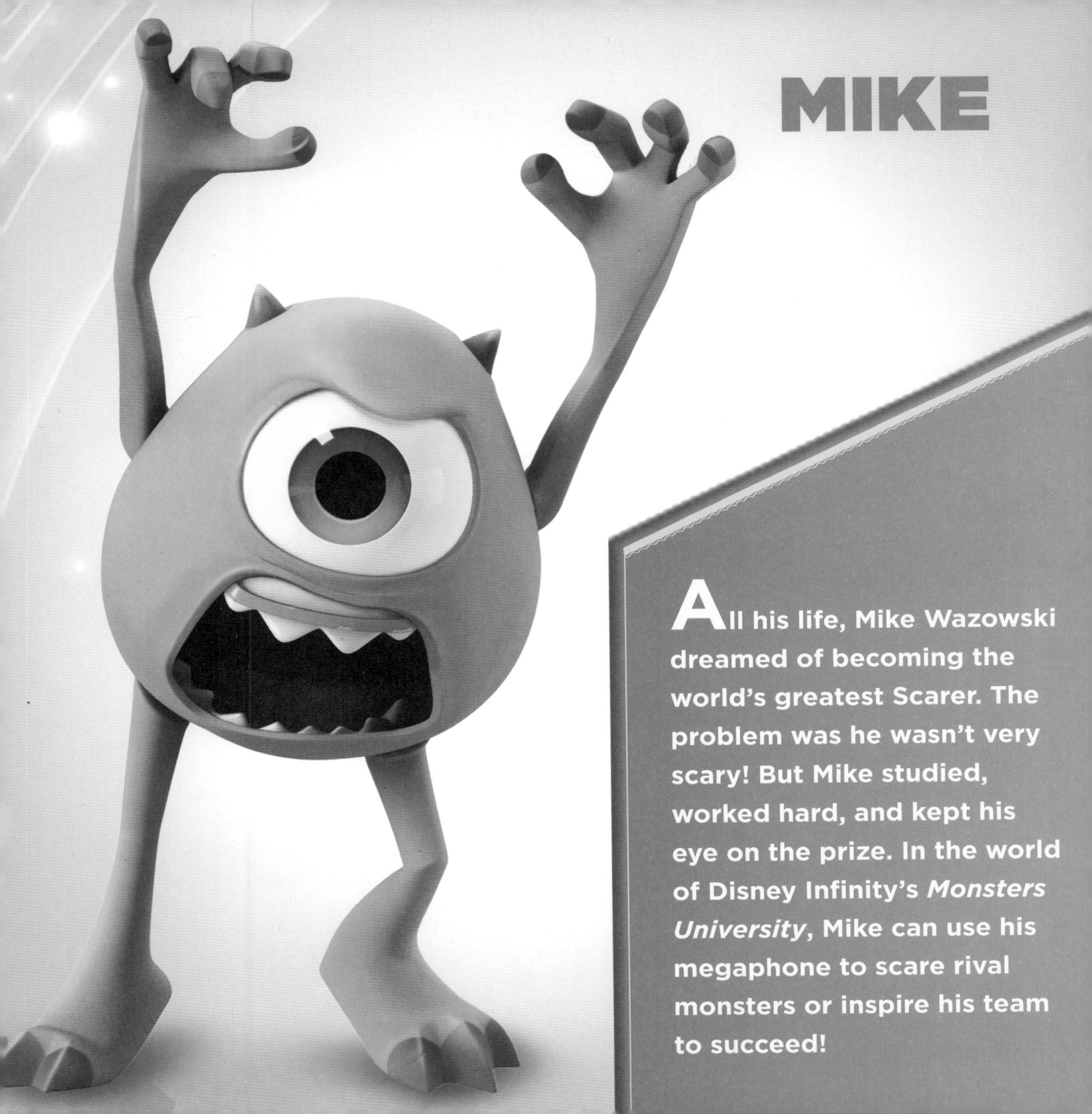

MIKE

All his life, Mike Wazowski dreamed of becoming the world's greatest Scarer. The problem was he wasn't very scary! But Mike studied, worked hard, and kept his eye on the prize. In the world of Disney Infinity's *Monsters University*, Mike can use his megaphone to scare rival monsters or inspire his team to succeed!

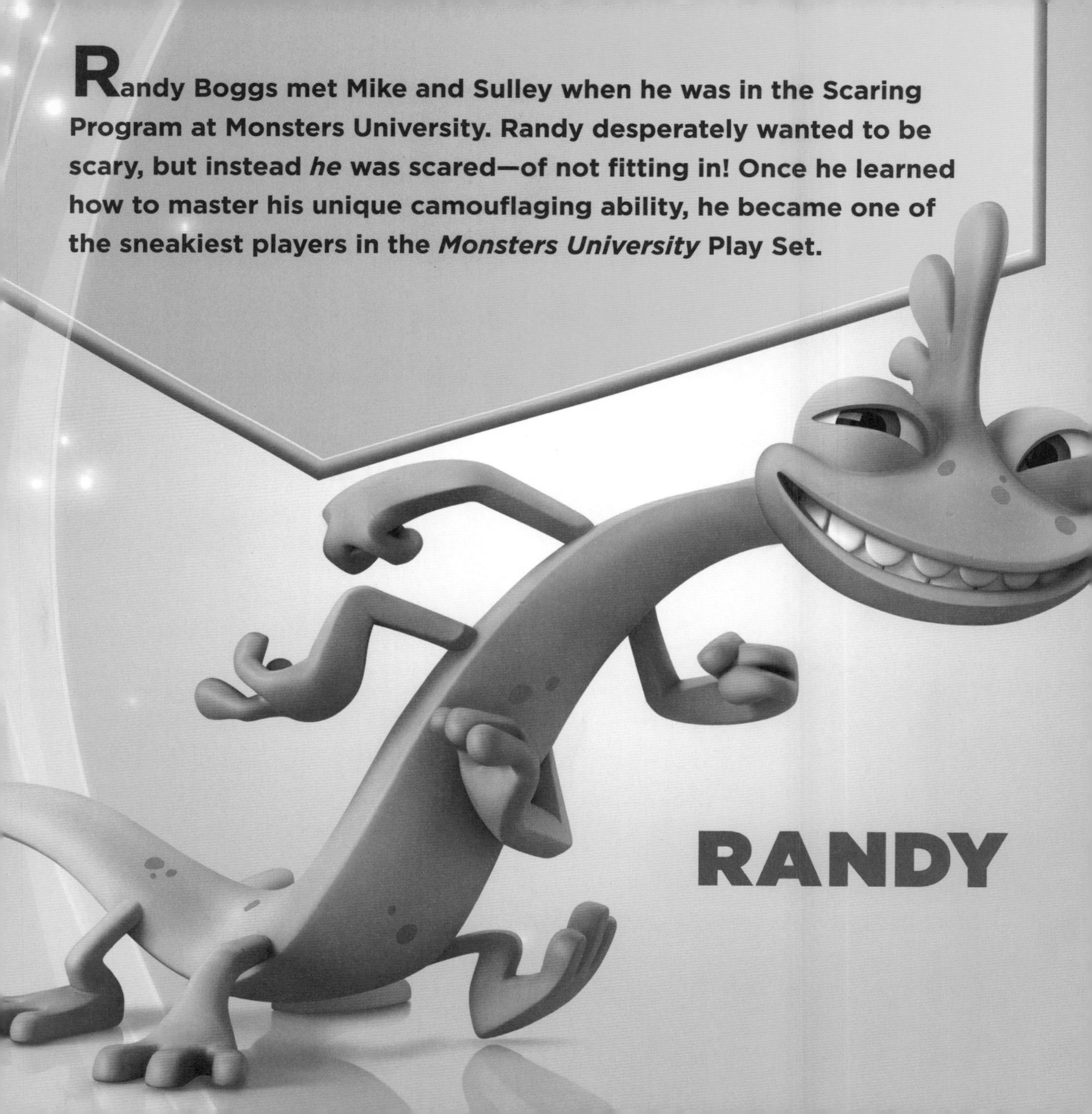

Randy Boggs met Mike and Sulley when he was in the Scaring Program at Monsters University. Randy desperately wanted to be scary, but instead *he* was scared—of not fitting in! Once he learned how to master his unique camouflaging ability, he became one of the sneakiest players in the *Monsters University* Play Set.

RANDY

SYNDROME

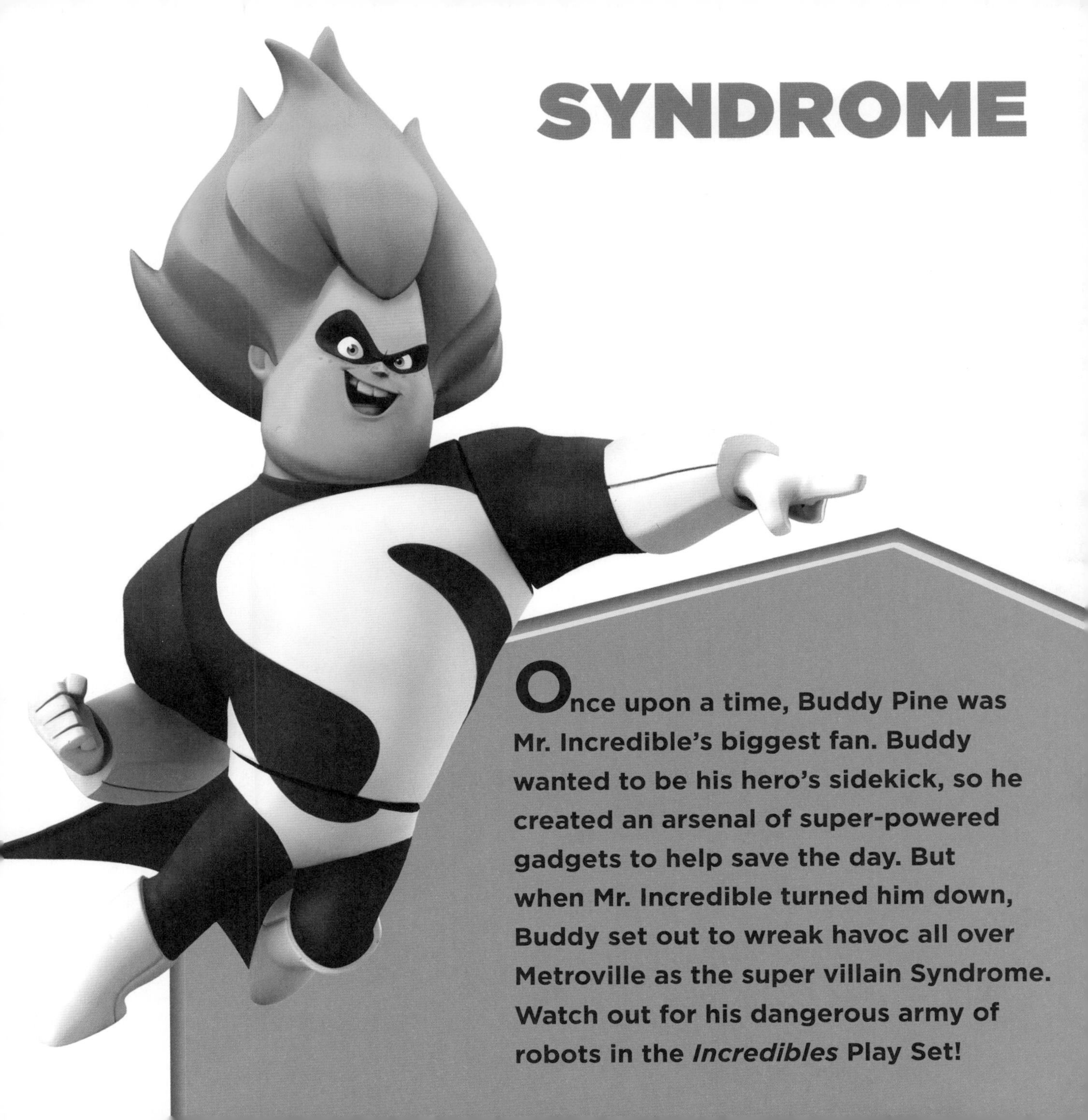

Once upon a time, Buddy Pine was Mr. Incredible's biggest fan. Buddy wanted to be his hero's sidekick, so he created an arsenal of super-powered gadgets to help save the day. But when Mr. Incredible turned him down, Buddy set out to wreak havoc all over Metroville as the super villain Syndrome. Watch out for his dangerous army of robots in the *Incredibles* Play Set!

MR. INCREDIBLE

Bob Parr belongs to a team of superheroes known as the Supers. Mr. Incredible is the strongest Super of all! He works tirelessly to defend his beloved city of Metroville. When Syndrome's mischief threatens his home, Mr. Incredible springs into action, using a combination of his super attacks to vanquish the villain!

MRS. INCREDIBLE

Mr. Incredible is not alone in his fight against Syndrome. Helen Parr, his wife, is also a member of the Supers. She uses her super-elastic skills to whip across town, pull objects closer together, swing up onto buildings, and keep her family of superheroes in line.

Violet Parr is a super-powered teenager and the daughter of Mr. and Mrs. Incredible. Violet can turn invisible and create force fields—abilities she uses to her advantage in the *Incredibles* Play Set! Violet is the perfect Super for sneaking up on bad guys.

VIOLET

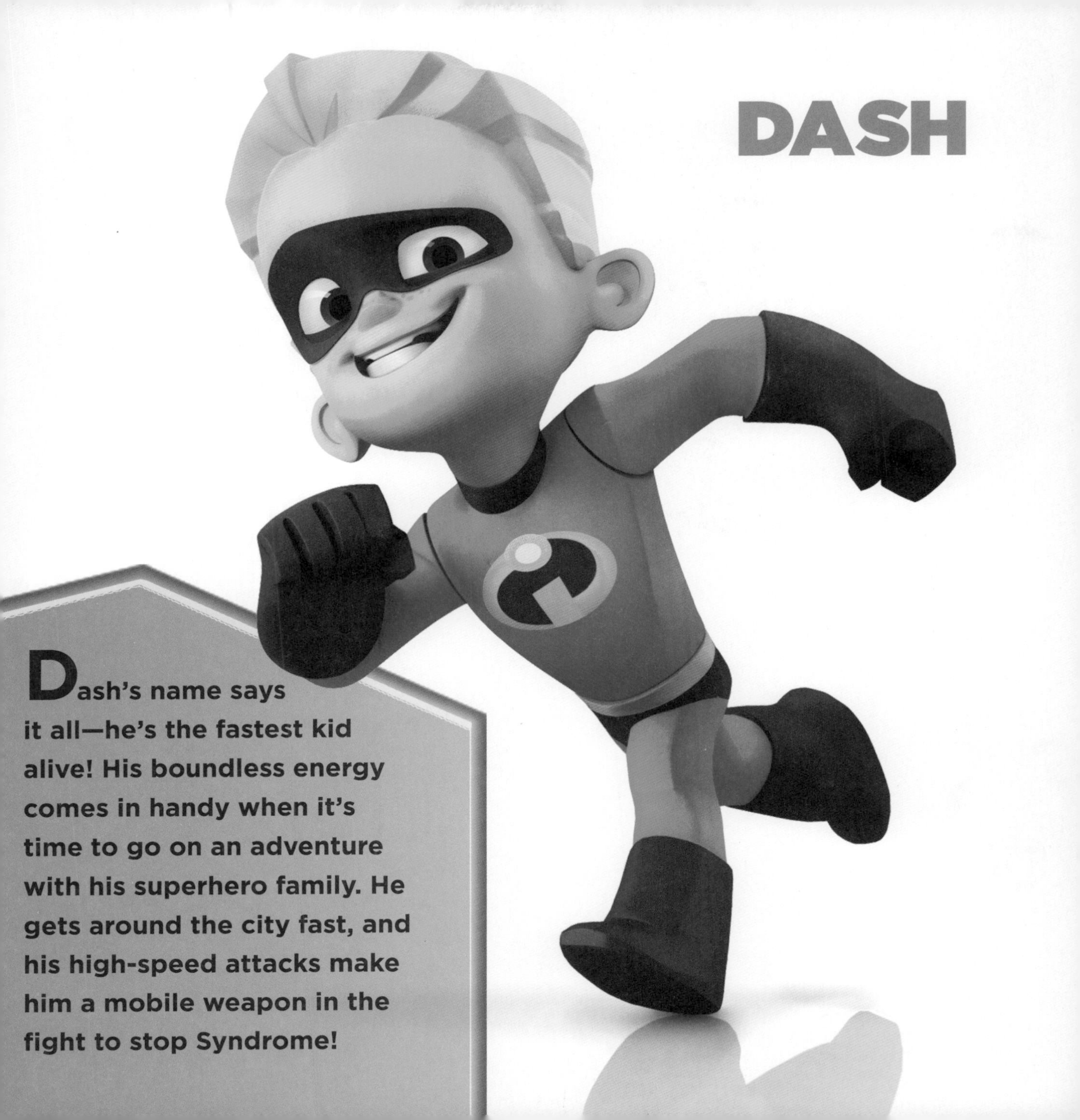

DASH

Dash's name says it all—he's the fastest kid alive! His boundless energy comes in handy when it's time to go on an adventure with his superhero family. He gets around the city fast, and his high-speed attacks make him a mobile weapon in the fight to stop Syndrome!

For as long as she can remember, Elsa has had the magical power to create and control ice. With the courage of a queen, Elsa can unleash a frosty freeze, making her a force to be reckoned with in the world of Disney Infinity!

ELSA

ANNA

Anna is an optimistic and fun-loving princess who lives in the kingdom of Arendelle. When her sister, Elsa, ran into trouble and left home, Anna stopped at nothing to bring her back. Anna may not have magical powers, but her running, jumping, and climbing abilities give her the skills she needs to take on any Toy Box challenge.

WRECK-IT RALPH

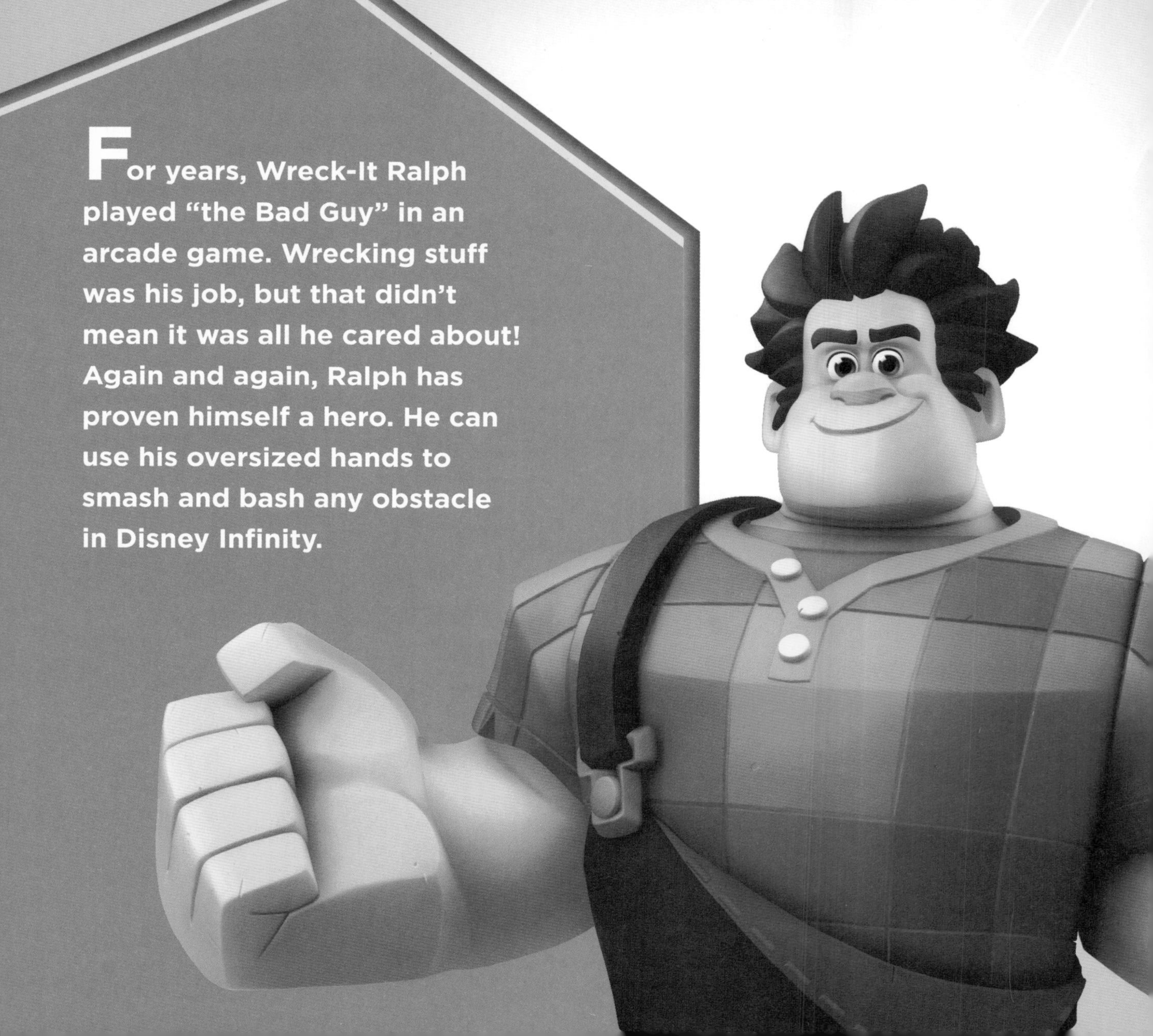

For years, Wreck-It Ralph played "the Bad Guy" in an arcade game. Wrecking stuff was his job, but that didn't mean it was all he cared about! Again and again, Ralph has proven himself a hero. He can use his oversized hands to smash and bash any obstacle in Disney Infinity.

© Disney
© Disney•Pixar
© Disney•Pixar
© Disney•Pixar
© Disney•Pixar
© Disney
DISNEY
INFINITY
© Disney•Pixar
© Disney•Pixar
© Disney
© Disney
© Disney•Pixar
© Disney
© Disney•Pixar
© Disney•Pixar
© Disney•Pixar
© Disney•Pixar
© Disney

© Disney
© Disney•Pixar
INFINITY
© Disney
DISNEY
© Disney•Pixar
© Disney
© Disney•Pixar
© Disney
© Disney•Pixar
© Disney•Pixar
© Disney
© Disney•Pixar
© Disney•Pixar
© Disney•Pixar
© Disney•Pixar
© Disney•Pixar
© Disney•Pixar

Because of her pixelating condition, poor Vanellope was called "the Glitch" by the other drivers in *Sugar Rush*, a candy-coated cart-racing video game. But Vanellope was made for speed. She can teleport glitch-style through any Disney Infinity adventure.

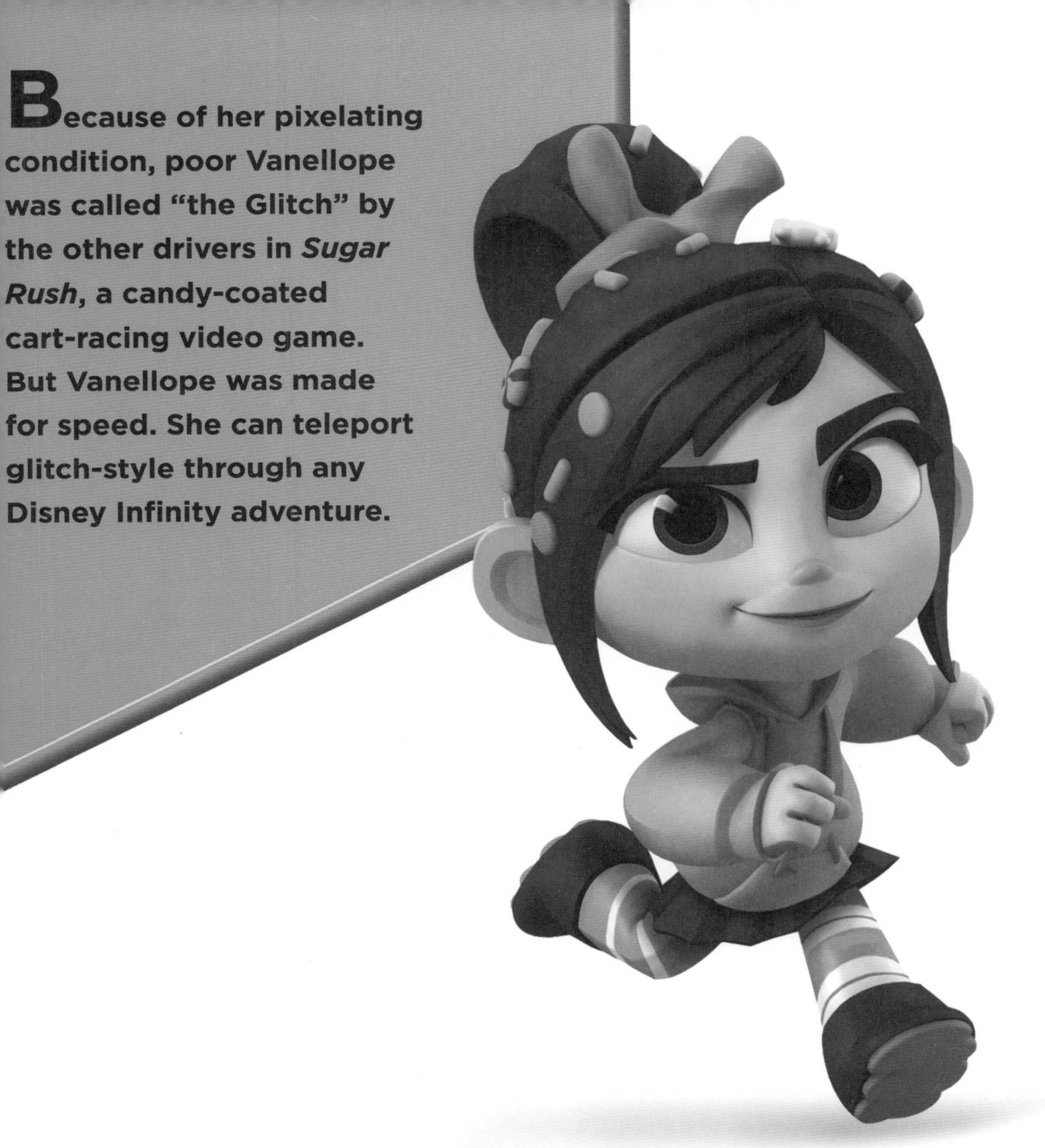

VANELLOPE VON SCHWEETZ

WOODY

Sheriff Woody is the leader of the toys in the *Toy Story* Play Set. He is courageous, clever, and kind to all characters. But bad guys and villains beware: Woody packs a shoulder charge that can blow any obstacle out of his way!

JESSIE

Jessie is a fun and friendly cowgirl doll who was an original member of Woody's Roundup gang. She loves playing pretend, and she has a horse named Bullseye. Jessie is always ready to ride into any Disney Infinity adventure!

Buzz Lightyear is a space ranger action figure whose bravery and combat skills always come in handy—especially on his adventures with his best pal, Woody. Wearing his super-charged jet pack, Buzz has the power to blast off, fly high, and go to Infinity and beyond!

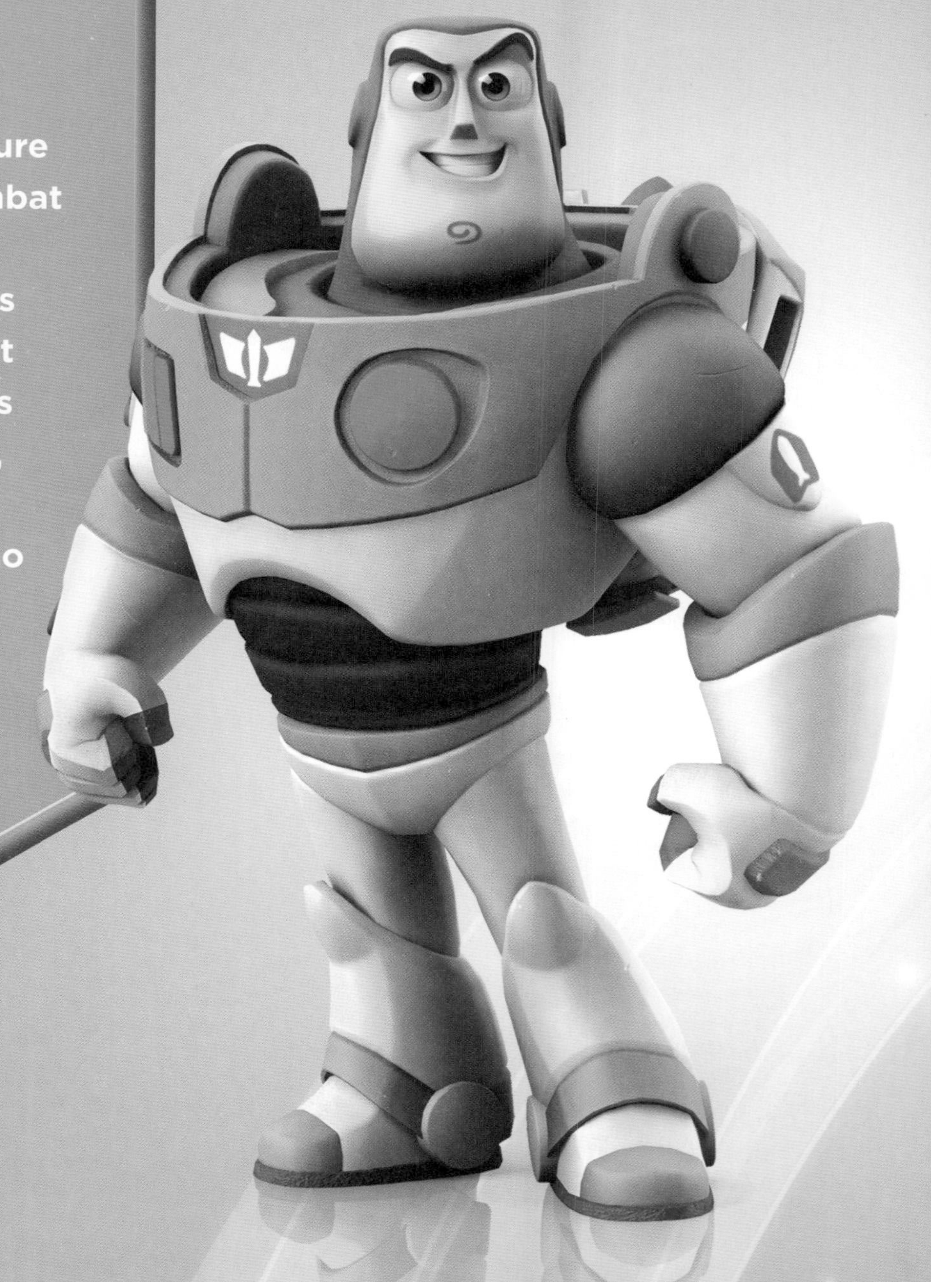

BUZZ LIGHTYEAR

Captain Jack Sparrow is a resourceful pirate captain. His wild journeys have led him across all of the Seven Seas. No matter where Captain Jack Sparrow finds himself in the Disney Infinity world, he's always ready to go on a bounty-finding treasure hunt or leap into a hearty sea battle!

CAPTAIN JACK SPARROW

BARBOSSA

Barbossa was once the first mate on Captain Jack Sparrow's ship, but then he led a mutiny and left Jack marooned on an island in the middle of the ocean. But Barbossa couldn't get away from the captain that easily—Sparrow escaped, and the two have been enemies ever since. Barbossa may be bad, but he's fun to play—and handy with a pirate bomb!

DAVY JONES

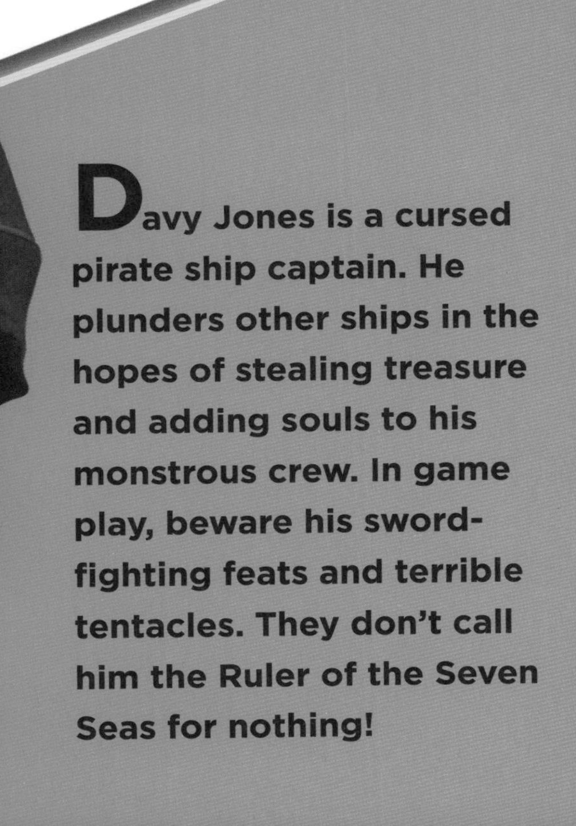

Davy Jones is a cursed pirate ship captain. He plunders other ships in the hopes of stealing treasure and adding souls to his monstrous crew. In game play, beware his sword-fighting feats and terrible tentacles. They don't call him the Ruler of the Seven Seas for nothing!

Lightning McQueen is a champion race car who has won four Piston Cups, and even competed in the first-ever World Grand Prix! Whether he's racing, jumping a canyon, or trailblazing through the desert, nothing slows him down in the world of Disney Infinity!

LIGHTNING McQUEEN

MATER

Mater, a good-natured tow truck, is Lightning McQueen's best buddy and number-one fan. The two friends have been on adventures all around the world. Mater might be a bit rusty, but he's got plenty of power under the hood! His amazing towing abilities make him one of the most helpful vehicles in the *Cars* Play Set.

Francesco Bernoulli is a Formula Racing champion and Europe's top-ranked race car. Fans love this shiny, showy speedster—but not as much as Francesco loves himself! He can zip around the *Cars* Play Set and still have enough fuel for showing off afterward. Better be careful, though—he's got hidden firepower under his hood!

FRANCESCO BERNOULLI

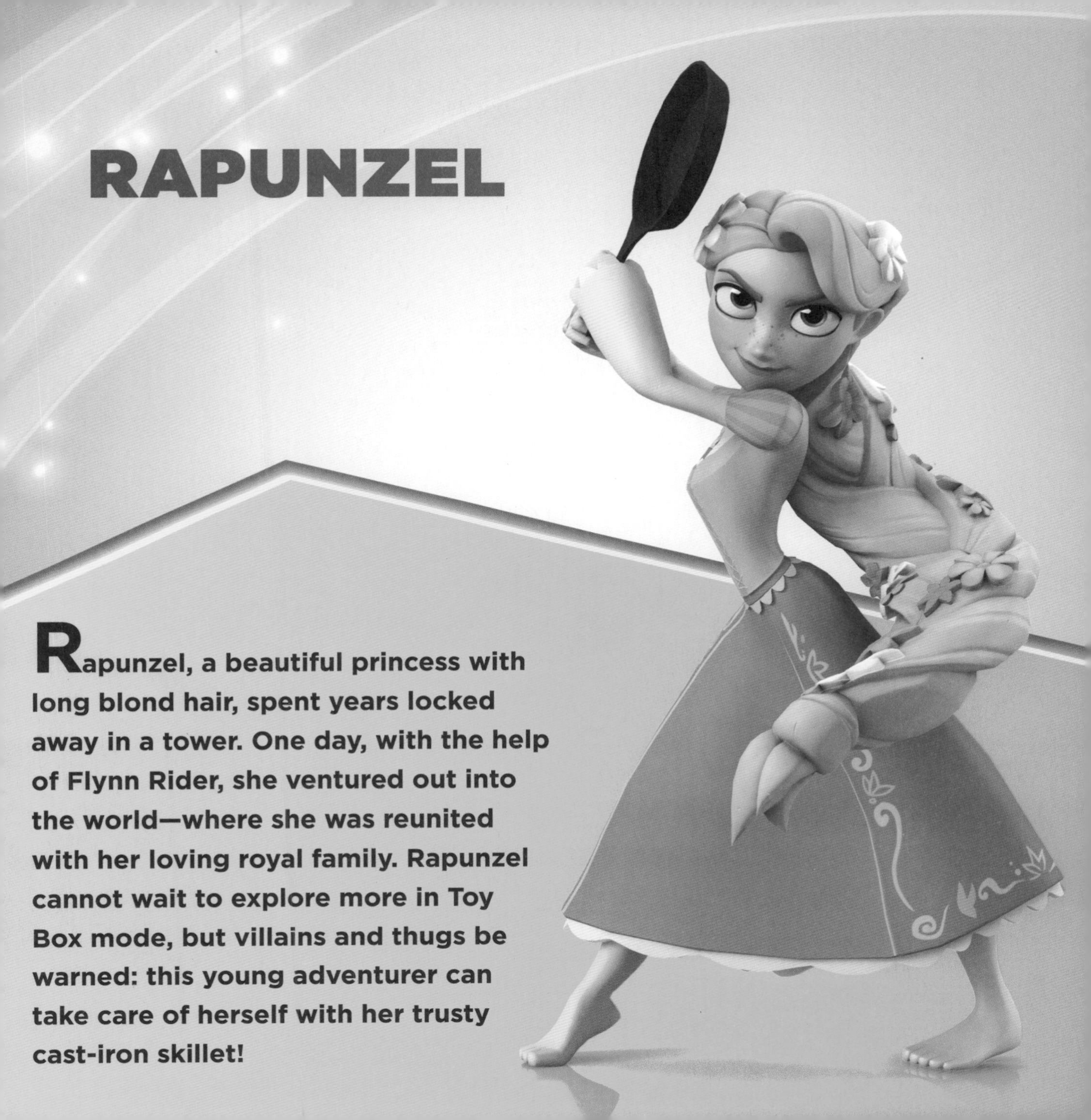

RAPUNZEL

Rapunzel, a beautiful princess with long blond hair, spent years locked away in a tower. One day, with the help of Flynn Rider, she ventured out into the world—where she was reunited with her loving royal family. Rapunzel cannot wait to explore more in Toy Box mode, but villains and thugs be warned: this young adventurer can take care of herself with her trusty cast-iron skillet!

Exciting adventures await you in the Disney Infinity world. Your imagination can take you on any magical journey you choose!